IAN FLEMING

CHITTY CHITTY BANG BANG

Adapted by **PETER BENTLY**

Illustrated by **STEVE ANTONY**

Jemima and Jeremy Pott lived by a lake with their mum and dad. They were a happy family, even though they were very poor.

But Dad was a clever inventor and one day he made some musical sweets that whistled when you sucked them. Everyone loved the sweets and Dad sold them for lots of money.

Suddenly the Potts were rich!

"Righto, let's go!" he said.
"Where?" chorused the others.
"To the garage," said Dad.
"We're going to buy a car!"

The Potts didn't like any of the cars at the garage.

But just as they were about to leave, Dad spotted something under a cover. It was a big old racing car, all rusty and broken.

"It's off to the scrapyard tomorrow," said the garage man.

"What a shame. It looks so sad," said Mum.

"Dad can fix it!" said Jeremy.

Dad shut himself up in his workshop to fix the old wreck.

For weeks and weeks, all the family heard was banging and hammering and scraping. The smell of oil and fresh paint drifted over the garden.

At last Dad said, "*Righto,* everybody! Come and meet our new car!"

The car looked **amazing**. Its paint shone.
Its headlights glistened and glinted.

"She's the most
beautiful car in the
world!" said Jemima.

Dad started the engine. It made two loud sneezes –

CHITTY! CHITTY!

– and two small explosions –

BANG! BANG!

– and thundered into life.

"She just told us her name," said Jeremy.
"It's **CHITTY-CHITTY-BANG-BANG!**"

"Let's go for a drive to the beach," said Mum. "It's such a lovely day."

Chitty-Chitty-Bang-Bang zoomed past all the other cars . . .

until she got stuck in a long traffic jam.

A knob flashed on the dashboard. It said **PULL ME!**

Dad pulled the knob. A propeller
popped out of the front of the car,
and the mudguards fanned out
like the wings of a bird. Then . . .

WHOOSH!

Chitty-Chitty-Bang-Bang soared into the sky.

"WOW!" cried the children. "She can FLY!"

"I knew this car was special!" laughed Dad.
"She's terrific!" said Mum.
"She's smashing!" said Jeremy.
"She's *magical!*" said Jemima.

When they got to the beach, there was nowhere to land. So CHITTY-CHITTY-BANG-BANG headed straight out to sea.

"Where are we going?" asked Mum.
"No idea," said Dad.
"Chitty is steering all by herself!"
"She's heading for that island!"
said Jeremy.
"Clever Chitty!" said Jemima.
"She's found an empty beach!"

Chitty-Chitty-Bang-Bang
landed smoothly, tucking
away her wings and propeller.

"Well done, Chitty!" said Mum.
Chitty's radiator hissed softly.
"She's saying, *'You're welcome',*" said Jemima.

The family had a lovely time on
the beach. They splashed in the
sea and ate a delicious picnic.

Afterwards they lay on the
golden sand and dozed
off in the sunshine.

They didn't see the sunshine turn to mist.
And that wasn't all . . .

GA-GOO-GA!

Chitty's klaxon horn woke Jeremy first. He cried out
in alarm. "Quickly, everyone! The tide's coming in!"

Mum started Chitty's engine.
"There's no room to take off!"
she said.

A button flashed on
the dashboard. It
said **PRESS ME!**

Mum pressed the button, and
Chitty's wheels swung out sideways.
"We're sinking!" cried Jemima.

But then the wheels began to spin, and in a moment
Chitty-Chitty-Bang-Bang was shooting through the waves.

"Brilliant!" declared Jeremy. "She's turned into a speedboat!"

It was hard to see where they were going.

At last the fog lifted and they saw the coast ahead.

"Look, it's France!" shouted Dad.
"What an adventure!"

Chitty's wheels clicked back
to normal and they bumped
their way up onto the shore.

Welcome to
FRANCE

"The tide is still coming in," said Mum.
"We can't stay on the beach."
"Look, a cave!" cried Jeremy.
"Perfect," said Mum.
"We can shelter in there."

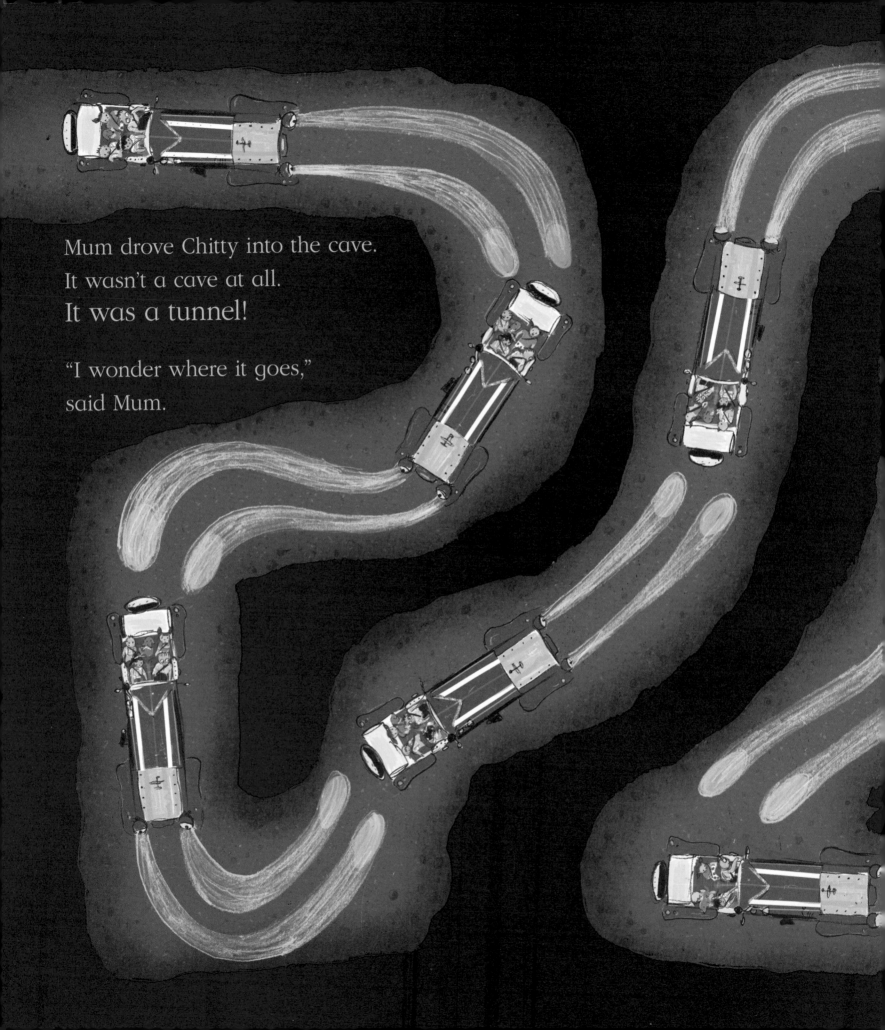

Mum drove Chitty into the cave.
It wasn't a cave at all.
It was a tunnel!

"I wonder where it goes,"
said Mum.

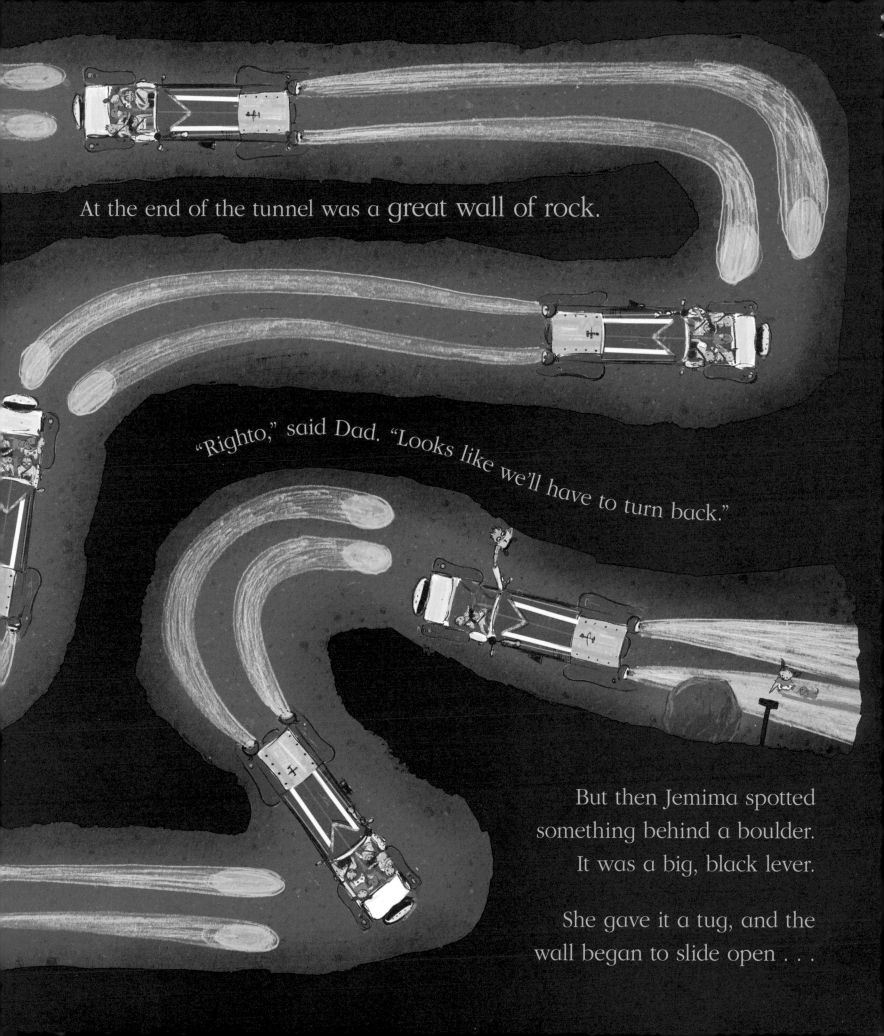

At the end of the tunnel was a great wall of rock.

"Righto," said Dad. "Looks like we'll have to turn back."

But then Jemima spotted
something behind a boulder.
It was a big, black lever.

She gave it a tug, and the
wall began to slide open . . .

Chitty's headlights lit up huge heaps of gold and jewels.

"Pirate treasure!" said Jemima.

Mum picked up a newspaper.

"Not pirates," she said.

"Robbers!"

JOE THE ROBBER STRIKES AGAIN!
Many Jewels Stolen in Paris

"This must be Joe the Robber's secret hideout!" said Dad.

"We should tell the police," said Mum.

On the other side of the hideout some people were unloading gold from a van.

"It's Joe the Robber!" said Jeremy.

Chitty blasted her horn.

GA-GOO-GA!

Joe yelled, "Quick! Scarper!"

The gang sped off in the van, out of the tunnel and onto
the motorway. "After them, Chitty!" cried Mum.
"Look, they're heading for Paris!" said Dad.

They chased the gang through
the city streets, but Chitty had
to stop at a traffic light.

"Bother," said Mum.
"We'll never catch them now."

The lights turned green and,
without warning, Chitty
swerved down a narrow alley.

"There's the van," said Jemima.
      "Clever Chitty!"

The robbers ran
into a park . . . .

They were heading straight for a hot-air balloon.

"They're escaping!" said Dad.

The knob on Chitty's dashboard began to flash: **PULL ME! PULL ME!**

PULL ME!

"Hold on tight!" said Mum.

She pulled the knob and once again Chitty flew up into the air.

"But how can we stop the balloon?" asked Jemima.

Chitty had the answer. She swooped
down and with her sharp wings –

SNIP-SNAP!

– she cut the ropes
of the balloon.

SPLASH!

The robbers tumbled into the river.

Chitty landed smoothly in the park.

As the police led the robbers away,
a smart limousine pulled up.

"Look, who's this?"
said Dad. "Surely it can't be . . ."

"It is!" said Mum. "It's the
President of France!"

The President shook their hands. "Thank you for catching the robbers!" she said. "As a reward, I am giving you this special medal."

"Thank you," said Jemima.
"But it isn't us who deserve
the medal . . ."

It's **CHITTY-CHITTY-**

To my Family, and the Spirit of Adventure. - P.B.

For Essie, Daphne, Velma and Nancy - S.A.

IAN FLEMING PUBLICATIONS LIMITED

HODDER CHILDREN'S BOOKS

First published in Great Britain in 2020 by Hodder and Stoughton
This paperback edition first published in Great Britain in 2022 by Hodder and Stoughton
Original text copyright © Ian Fleming Publications Ltd 1964, 1965
Text adaptation copyright © Ian Fleming Publications Ltd 2020
Illustrations copyright © Ian Fleming Publications Ltd 2020
The moral rights of the author and illustrator have been asserted.
All rights reserved.

Chitty Chitty Bang Bang is a registered trademark of Danjaq LLC and United Artists
Corporation, used under licence by Ian Fleming Publications Ltd. All rights reserved.

The Ian Fleming Logo and the Ian Fleming Signature are both trademarks owned by
The Ian Fleming Estate, used under licence by Ian Fleming Publications Ltd.

A CIP catalogue record of this book
is available from the British Library.

HB ISBN: 978 1 444 94820 2
PB ISBN: 978 1 444 94821 9

1 3 5 7 9 10 8 6 4 2

Printed and bound in China.

Hodder Children's Books
An imprint of
Hachette Children's Group
Part of Hodder and Stoughton
Carmelite House
50 Victoria Embankment
London EC4Y 0DZ

An Hachette UK Company
www.hachette.co.uk
www.hachettechildrens.co.uk